This Topsy and Tim
book belongs to

_____

Topsy and Tim
Help a Friend

By Jean and Gareth Adamson
Consultants: The Anti-Bullying Alliance

LADYBIRD BOOKS

UK | USA | Canada | Ireland | Australia
India | New Zealand | South Africa

Ladybird Books is part of the Penguin Random House group of companies
whose addresses can be found at global.penguinrandomhouse.com
www.penguin.co.uk   www.puffin.co.uk   www.ladybird.co.uk

First published by Ladybird Books Ltd, 2005
This edition 2015
004

Printed in China

A CIP catalogue record for this book is available from the British Library

ISBN: 978–0–723–29259–3

All correspondence to:
Ladybird Books
Penguin Random House Children's
80 Strand, London WC2R 0RL

The Anti-Bullying Alliance are happy to support *Topsy and Tim: Help a Friend* to help young
children understand bullying and what they can do to help stop the bullies.

One morning, Topsy and Tim met Stevie Dunton
at the school gate. Stevie looked upset.
"What's wrong, Stevie?" asked Tim.
"I hate school," said Stevie.

Stevie cheered up when they went into the classroom,
but at break he didn't want to go out to play.
"What's wrong, Stevie?" asked Miss Terry.
"Nothing," said Stevie, and he went outside.

Topsy and Tim were playing 'It' in the playground
with their friends. Kerry was 'It'. Stevie joined in and
Kerry began to chase him.

Stevie was a good runner. He was getting away
from Kerry when James, the biggest boy in the class,
stuck out his foot and tripped Stevie up.

Stevie began to cry.

"Cry baby, cry baby!" shouted James and his friend, Sylvie.

Some of the children laughed. Topsy and Tim didn't,
but they didn't know what to do.

After break, it was P.E. The children had to change into
their plimsolls. Soon, everyone was ready except Stevie.
"Come on, Stevie, we're waiting for you," said Miss Terry.
"I can't find one of my plimsolls," said Stevie.

"There it is!" said Topsy, pointing to Stevie's peg.
"How did it get there?" said Stevie.
Tim saw Sylvie wink at James.

After school, Topsy and Tim told Mummy about
James and Sylvie.
"James keeps on being nasty to Stevie," said Topsy.
"And Sylvie copies him," said Tim.
"I think Sylvie and James are being bullies," said Mummy.
"What's a bully?" asked Topsy.

"It's someone who likes to hurt or frighten other people," said Mummy. "They make everyone afraid to tell a grown-up. It was brave of you to tell me, and you should tell Miss Terry, too."

"But that's telling tales," said Topsy.
"That's what bullies think," said Mummy. "That's how they get away with hurting other people."

When Stevie was hanging up his coat the next day at school, James ran in. He grabbed Stevie's school bag and threw it across the room.
"Catch, Sylvie!" he shouted.

"That's not yours!" shouted Topsy.
"Give it back to Stevie," yelled Tim.
Sylvie grabbed the bag and threw it back to James.

James dropped the bag on the floor and
everything fell out. Everyone laughed,
except Topsy and Tim and Stevie.

"What's going on in here?" asked Miss Terry.
"James did it," said Topsy. "He's always doing nasty things to Stevie."
"He's a bully," said Tim.

"All right, children, calm down," said Miss Terry.
"I think it's time we had a class chat."

When all the children were settled,
Miss Terry talked to them about bullying.
Then, she asked them to tell her what bullies did.

"They hit you and hurt you," said Andy Anderson.
"They call you names," said Rai.
"They make your friends be nasty to you,"
said Louise.
"They think it's funny and don't always know they
are hurting your feelings," said Alice.

"Why are bullies so unkind?" asked Topsy. "Sometimes bullies have been bullied themselves," said Miss Terry. "Then, they take it out on someone else because it makes them feel big." Topsy and Tim began to feel sorry for the bullies.

"I hate bullying!" said Kerry.
"Does anyone here like bullying?" asked Miss Terry.
"NO!" shouted all the children.

At lunch, Miss Terry, James, Sylvie and Stevie Dunton sat down to have a chat.

"I'm sorry I've been mean to you," said James, looking upset.

"Me, too," said Sylvie. "We don't want to be bullies."

"Thank you for saying sorry," said Stevie. "You did upset me, but let's be friends instead."

Everyone played 'It' together. Soon, it was time to go back into the classroom.

"You look like you've been playing nicely," said Miss Terry.

"We've had lots of fun!" said Tim.

After school, Topsy and Tim and Stevie ran to the school gates to meet their mums.

"Was school all right today?" asked Stevie's mum.

"Yes, it was," said Stevie. "I've got something to tell you."

Stevie told his mum that James and Sylvie had been bullying him.

"Oh, dear!" said Stevie's mum, looking upset.
"Don't worry, Mum," said Stevie. "Topsy and Tim told Miss Terry about it and she talked to the whole class. I feel much better because James and Sylvie said they were sorry, too."
Stevie's mum gave him a big hug.

"Goodbye, Stevie," said Topsy and Tim. "See you tomorrow."
Stevie smiled and waved at them.
"See you tomorrow," he called. "I can't wait for school now."

*Now turn the page and help
Topsy and Tim solve a puzzle.*

Look at the two pictures of the children playing 'It' in the playground. There are six tricky differences between the pictures. Can you spot them all?

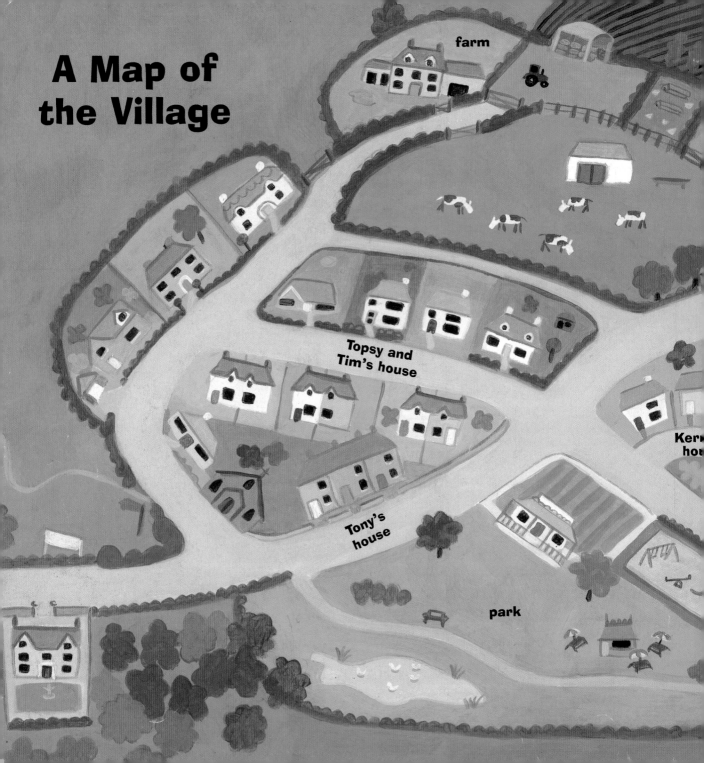

A Map of the Village

farm

Topsy and Tim's house

Tony's house

Kerr house

park

garage

health centre

post office

church

primary school

nursery school

police station

Have you read all the Topsy and Tim stories?

 The New Baby
☐ 9781409300564

 Have a Birthday Party
☐ 9781409300618

 Go on an Aeroplane
☐ 9781409300571

 Play Football
☐ 9781409303350

 Go on a Train
☐ 9781409304241

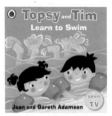 Learn to Swim
☐ 9781409300601

 Start School
☐ 9781409300830

 Go Camping
☐ 9781409303336

 Go to Hospital
☐ 9781409304234

 Go to the Zoo
☐ 9781409300847

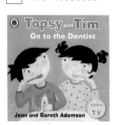 Go to the Dentist
☐ 9781409300588

 At the Farm
☐ 9781409303367

 Go to the Doctor
☐ 9781409303343

 Have Itchy Heads
☐ 9781409307204

 Meet the Firefighters
☐ 9781409307211

 Safety First
☐ 9781409308829

 Meet the Police
☐ 9781409308836

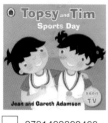 Sports Day
☐ 9781409309468

 Visit London
☐ 9781409309475

 Meet Father Christmas
☐ 9781409311591

 Help a Friend
☑ 9780723292593

 Move House
☐ 9780723292586

 First Sleepover
☐ 9780241189702

 Have Their Eyes Tested
☐ 9780241282540

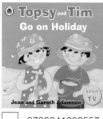 Go on Holiday
☐ 9780241282557